The New Football Coach

Dominique Demers

Translated by Sander Berg

Illustrations by Tony Ross

ALMA JUNIOR

ALMA BOOKS LTD
3 Castle Yard
Richmond
Surrey TW10 6TF
United Kingdom
www.almajunior.com

The Mysterious Librarian first published in French by Éditions Québec
Amérique in 2007
This translation first published by Alma Books Ltd in 2018
© Dominique Demers, 2007

Translation © Sander Berg, 2018

Inside and cover illustrations by Tony Ross. Illustrations first published
in France by Éditions Gallimard Jeunesse
© Éditions Gallimard Jeunesse, 2008

Printed in Great Britain by CPI Group (UK) Ltd, Croydon CR0 4YY

ISBN: 978-1-84688-435-1

The New Football Coach

Contents

The New Football Coach

Chapter 1

Yvette Pesky's Challenge

When I saw her coming, I nearly did a runner. I was not expecting THAT, even though my cousin Marie had warned me: "You'll see, Jeremy: Miss Charlotte is very... different."

Let's just say I had not expected her to be *that* different. Marie had not mentioned that Miss Charlotte was tall and as thin as an asparagus, that she was everything but a spring chicken and that she wore weird clothes and a huge hat, a bit like a witch's hat but with a round top instead of a pointy one.

I have nothing against being original. The problem was that Miss Charlotte had not been invited to a fancy-dress party. She had come to rescue us. To save our skins. That's how I saw it at least.

Her mission was straightforward: to train the players of the Black Duck Brook Football Club. *My* club. And we simply *had* to beat the team from Blueberry Bay in the last match of the season. And if I say we *had* to, I am not exaggerating. And THAT is of course the problem…

Our headmistress, Paulette Pesky, is the twin sister of Yvette Pesky, the headmistress of the Blueberry Bay school. The two headmistresses have been bickering since they were in nursery school – or as good as – and they still argue over everything. This time they both want their school to be named after the famous international football star Tony Brilliant. Tony Brilliant lives in England now, but he was born in between Black Duck Brook and Blueberry Bay.

We, the pupils, could not care less. Renaming the school will not change our lives in the least. Still, we are in a real fix!

A few weeks ago, Yvette Pesky challenged her sister and our headmistress Paulette: the school that would win the last match of the season could call itself the Tony Brilliant School. Ever since then, every day at half-eight, Paulette Pesky hollers down the PA system: "Victory will be ours! We must win!" When I hear that, I feel my stomach tying itself into knots.

Our opponents have found a fearsome coach: Reginald Robust, Yvette Pesky's husband, an ex-Army colonel, super-strict, mega-disciplined

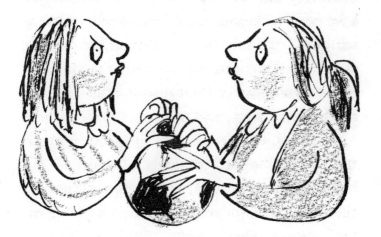

and ever so determined. He will do anything to win.

On hearing the news, our coach, Ed Coward, handed in his notice. And no one is willing to replace him. Everyone is too scared to take on Reginald Robust!

The day our coach dropped us like a hot brick, I rang my cousin Marie. I needed to speak to someone I could trust. As she had done on previous occasions, Marie talked about a certain Miss Charlotte, who has changed her life. That's when we came up with a plan.

Marie rang Paulette Pesky pretending to be a headmistress who could recommend her a football coach. My cousin is a great actress. She sang Miss Charlotte's praises so much that PP – that is what we call our headmistress – hired her without even meeting her!

All we had to do now was to track down that supposedly wonderful Miss Charlotte. One little problem, though: she does not have an address! Marie suggested leaving a message on the Grapevine website. And it worked! Although

I don't really understand how. The message sounded like code to me. I only remember it had something to do with a certain Gertrude.

But none of that matters now. What is important is that we must do well in the last match of the season. If we don't, it will be *so* embarrassing. If we get thrashed, hundreds of spectators will laugh at us. And not just the supporters of the other team! My neighbours, my parents, my mates and all the girls in the school will see us being utterly defeated. And that is not the worst! The worst is that my dad will tell me that he is disappointed, and he'll go on about it for weeks, if not years. And that really would be too embarrassing.

I hate football for a million good reasons. Firstly, because I am rubbish at it. Proper rubbish. As in no good, hopeless, useless – a complete disaster. If I had the choice, I would play chess, not football. What I am good at is strategy. I am really good at coming up with tactics and predicting how the opponent will attack, and then outsmarting them. Unfortunately for me, my dad is mad about football and owns a shop called Sports Plus. He was the one who forced Ed Coward to take me on his team.

It's my dad's fault that I am bombarded with insults from Fred Ferocio, the team's top scorer and a right pain in the neck. What he is best at? Shouting at the top of his voice and in front of all the girls: "Jeremy Catastrophe!"

Yesterday, when Fred saw Miss Charlotte enter the gym, he did not for a second think that she could possibly be our new coach. Nor did the others. My teammates kept on asking me questions about that mysterious Miss Charlotte, and they were all anxious to meet her. Had she played in a top league? Had she coached a famous team?

I did not know what to say. My cousin was convinced that her old teacher was the best person on the planet for the job, but she had not explained why. I was about to make up some story when this weird lady stood still in front of us. That beanstalk of a woman with her bizarre headgear, could *she* be our new coach? My stomach tied itself into one huge knot.

She stopped and just smiled, calmly looking at us with her blue, cheerful eyes. After a few seconds in which we all stood there gawping, Priti, the fastest player in the team and also the most polite, asked her: "Can we help you?" The celery stick answered: "Oh no, I have come to help *you*!" After that, she did a funny pirouette followed by a curtsy, like they do in films when they greet a king or a queen. Then she declared: "I am Miss Charlotte, your new football coach!"

Ten pairs of eyes turned to me, shooting daggers. I had the impression that the team would have preferred to have our headmistress, the dreaded PP herself, have a go at coaching our team. I was sure they were about to chop me into little pieces when Miss Charlotte announced: "Today we will be learning how to lose."

That is literally what she said! My teammates were so shocked that they forgot all about smashing me to a pulp.

They were stunned, and all they could do was listen to what she had to say.

Chapter 2

Smalalamiam, Anyone?

She was not joking. Miss Charlotte's objective for our first training session was that we had to learn how to lose! But first she had to convince Fred Ferocio to join us on the pitch.

"When you play football," she explained, "there is usually one team that wins and another one that loses. So it is very important to learn how to lose. Victory is great, but defeat could be even better!"

Fred interrupted her. "OK, enough of playing the clown! YOU may have learnt how to lose, but WE know how to play and we are here to WIN. If you are in any doubt, go and talk to PP."

We all agreed with Fred. There was a brief silence. As Laurence, the team's joker, always says: you could hear an ant pant.

"Do you know how to play?" asked Miss Charlotte, not sounding convinced. "Show me, then!"

We all leapt to our feet. Except for Fred.

"On one condition," he said, trying to strike a deal. "First show us that *you* know how to play. Let's just say that you don't look like you can."

Many of my team-mates burst out laughing. But Miss Charlotte paid no attention. "Yay!" she shouted, clapping in her hands like an excited child.

We left the gym to walk onto the pitch. Only now did I notice that our new coach was carrying a bag made of goodness knows what kind of leather. And from it she took a football. It looked like an ordinary football. I sighed with relief. And then Miss Charlotte said: "Let me introduce you to… Anatole!"

At that point we all felt like skedaddling. Except that we did not have the time, because

Miss Charlotte had started to play with Anatole. She played like a pro and put on quite a show! She let the ball roll from one shoulder to the other and juggled it using her head, her knees, her back and even her backside… Fred's eyes were like saucers.

"Where did you learn to do that?" asked Laurence when Miss Charlotte had stopped, her eyes shining and not the least bit out of breath.

"Oh well, Anatole and I go back a long time…"

Ten minutes after we started our game, our new coach scored her third goal. Not only did she play well, it was obvious how much fun she was having. It was as if in the whole wide world there were nothing better than to run after a black-and-white ball.

Normally coaches *watch* their teams. They are there to observe, to criticize, to shout orders, to offer advice… and to give players who make mistakes an earful. I know, because I have had plenty!

Miss Charlotte was different. For starters, when we formed two teams, she insisted on playing herself. Her team won, making Fred furious. He had just suffered a rare defeat, while I found myself on the winning side, which was unheard of!

Miss Charlotte's enthusiasm had the effect of a magic potion on us. I nearly forgot how much I hated the game. She laughed and joked and encouraged us. Every player surpassed him- or herself. The second match was won by Fred's team. He had never played better.

At the end of our training session, Miss Charlotte put Anatole carefully back in her bag, caressing the ball softly. As if it were alive!

"Now let's decide who was the man or woman of the match," our new coach proposed. "Who should get that honour, you think?"

Everyone turned their eyes to Fred, who was already putting on a triumphant smile. No need to say he had scored the most goals.

"Him? No, no. I don't see why. I want to know who *lost* the best," Miss Charlotte said.

No one said a word. We were wondering if our coach did it on purpose to provoke us, or if she was a bit off her rocker.

"Just have a think about it. Tomorrow I will treat those who come up with the best answer to some smalalamiam."

And whoosh! Off she went.

A thousand questions were milling around in my head. What was smalalamiam? What does it mean to "lose the best"? And could anyone actually *prefer* to lose?

Normally, after a training, all the players are in a hurry to go home. They are tired and hungry, and they have tons of homework to be getting on with, mates to see and TV series to watch. This time, it was different. We stayed behind to see Miss Charlotte walk off with her funny leather bag in which she kept Anatole.

That is when I found myself thinking that perhaps Anatole was a magic football. That with any other ball Miss Charlotte would have been useless. Like me! It was also when I discovered that I was looking forward to our next training session. And that, to be honest, was the most amazing thing of all.

Chapter 3

Somebody Pinch Me, Please!

The next day, all the pupils in school had heard of Anatole. And of Miss Charlotte! I told my friend Billy about our first training session, and he promised he would come to the next one.

Poor Billy Bungalow. He is as unhappy as I am, but for opposite reasons. He would give anything to be part of the team. My friend Billy is a real boffin, but he is about as fast as a snail and does not really have the body of an athlete. Let's just say he is on the chubby side – no doubt because he eats too many toffees. As soon as he gets bored, he whips out a toffee!

Plus, his dad does not own a sports shop. So, understandably, he never made the team.

I had been thinking a lot about the mystery surrounding Miss Charlotte, but I had come no closer to resolving it. Everyone knows that you are a bad loser if you smash the place up because you have lost. But no one lost their temper yesterday. So how could we have lost *better*? I mentioned it to Billy, who said he would give it some thought.

That day, for the first time, people had come to watch the training session. And not just Billy. I also saw Fiona Falbala, a Barbie doll who always flutters her eyelids at Fred Ferocio. Miranda and Monica, two friends of Fiona's who are more interested in boys than in football, were there too, as well as a dozen or so other children.

Miss Charlotte was the last to arrive. She walked towards us, put her bag down and gave us a beaming smile. The kind of smile that warms you on the inside. And that was just what I needed! The night before, during dinner, my dad had given me a speech that had shaken my confidence.

"Jeremy, listen to me. On the day of the match I expect you to do well. Understood? Don't forget that your father owns the Sports Plus shop. You have to score at least one goal. Am I making myself clear?"

He made himself clear enough, all right. My ears were buzzing and my heart skipped a beat.

"And? Has anyone come up with an answer?" Miss Charlotte asked.

A voice rang out from the stands. It was Billy!

"There is no right answer," he declared. "No one lost best, because everyone did an excellent job. Jeremy told me that..."

Miss Charlotte's face lit up, and she smiled so radiantly that it seemed she was glowing from within.

"Bravo, Billy!" she exclaimed.

She knew my friend's name! Since when? Feeling encouraged, Billy continued: "Losing

well is perhaps just the same as winning well. You just need to do your best. Give it all you can."

Miss Charlotte was over the moon. She started to jump up and down and let out little cries of excitement, as if Billy had pulled off some really difficult task.

"You are absolutely right," she said, once she had calmed down a little. "All of you were star players yesterday."

Then she added, looking at Billy: "But why don't you play too?"

Billy lowered his eyes.

"Because I didn't get picked," he answered, looking ashamed of himself.

Miss Charlotte did not seem to understand. She turned to us, as if expecting an explanation. My eyes met Fred's. He looked disgusted.

"Billy is rubbish," Fred said. "That's all there is to it. Like Jeremy! But let's not go there…"

The worst thing, the most astonishing thing, was that Miss Charlotte did not seem to understand his answer at all.

"Would you like to be in the team?" she finally asked Billy.

Billy swallowed hard. "Yes," he replied with a tiny voice. Then he got a grip on himself and added, more loudly: "I would love to."

"Well then, you have been officially selected!" our coach said, as if no one could possibly object.

Behind me, Fred Ferocio blurted out furiously: "Somebody pinch me, please! I can't believe this is actually happening."

Miss Charlotte did not let herself be intimidated, and asked: "Who else wants to join the team?"

A few minutes later, the number of players had doubled. Even Fiona Falbala, who is always afraid of breaking her nails, had come down from the stands. It was as if Miss Charlotte had hypnotized them all.

We formed two teams and then we played. As simple as that. Like the day before, there was something magic in the air.

Normally, I make one mistake after the next on the pitch – a true klutz. As soon as I get

near the ball, it seems to develop a will of its own. But that day, I played well. No one shouted at me or hurled insults at me. To my great surprise, I managed to get the ball twice. Not that I scored, of course. But as Miss Charlotte says, that is not the most important part.

That day, I played in the same team as Fred. We were ahead in the match with three goals to two when Miss Charlotte kicked the football off the field. That happens a lot during a game – it's normal. But this time it was different. Miss Charlotte did it on purpose. There was no doubt about it!

There she stood, in the middle of the pitch, with her arms dangling next to her and her eyes fixed on the horizon. She looked ecstatic, as if she were seeing something from another dimension.

"What a magnificent sunset!" she exclaimed after a while.

And the sky did in fact look gorgeous. Fred Ferocio, however, did not give a fig.

"I don't know what planet you come from, but we are training in order to win a match that will take place next month. And if we continue like this, we will get thrashed by the other team. They have a *real* coach, one who shouts, who criticizes and who tells his players what to do and even what to eat."

Fred was all het up. He paused for a second to regain his breath, and then he continued: "Do you know Reginald Robust makes his players drink a special drink twice a day? Someone told me about this. It contains yak milk, raw eggs, protein powder, vitamin granules and some sort of Chinese root."

We were devastated. We had been having a good time, but we had forgotten about the important event ahead: the match against the school from Blueberry Bay! Fred might be cut out to take them on, but not me. Nor Billy, or Fiona, or…

"Yak milk? Hah! They can drink gorilla milk, for all I care. Nothing beats smalalamiam!" declared Miss Charlotte with great confidence.

Smalalamiam! We had forgotten all about it.

Miss Charlotte extracted a bottle from her bag. Billy had earned the right to have the first taste. He took a gulp. Then another. And another.

"And?" asked Laurence.

Billy wiped his mouth and said: "This is the best drink I have ever had!"

Chapter 4

I Love You Lots, Anatole

At the weekend I spoke to my cousin Marie. She wanted to know everything that had happened with Miss Charlotte. Marie promised she and her dad would be at the last match of the season. Even though they live hours and hours by car away. She was absolutely desperate to see her friend Charlotte again – and to give her back a precious object, she added mysteriously.

Marie admitted that Pauline Pesky had rung her up at home after meeting Miss Charlotte in her office. Luckily Marie had a day off school, so she was the one who picked up the phone. Had her mum or dad answered the call, PP would have discovered she had been had.

Our headmistress was very worried. Not only did Miss Charlotte's appearance inspire little confidence, but the new coach had said some odd things at their first meeting. When PP had asked her what the secret of success was, she had replied: "*Spling*!" When Miss Charlotte had left the office, PP looked the word up in her dictionary, only to discover it does not actually exist!

When I spoke to Marie, I explained that PP was not the only one to ask questions about Miss Charlotte. Some parents had seen her having a picnic on the lawn in front of the church, in the middle of town. No one else had ever dared to have a picnic there! And Miss Charlotte had done more than just tuck into a sandwich in the main square. She had spread out a chequered sheet, placed a pretty vase with flowers next to her, lit a few candles and put out various dishes. All the passers-by stopped and stared, but she did not seem to notice.

After lessons on Monday, Billy and I changed into our football kit as quick as a flash and went to the gym. It was raining too hard to play outside. When we opened the door, we heard Miss Charlotte's voice. I thought she was talking to PP. But when we got nearer we discovered our coach was deep in conversation with... her football!

"Do you think they will understand? Yes, you are right. We just need to give them time."

Miss Charlotte sighed and stroked her football with her fingertips.

"I love you lots, Anatole," she added. "But I do miss my beautiful Gertrude…"

I heard some people chuckle behind me. Other pupils had come in and heard Miss Charlotte talking to Anatole. I was embarrassed for her. But Miss Charlotte did not seem to mind a bit.

"I am so happy to see you!" she cried out. "So is Anatole. We were just having a nice chat."

"A chat with your football?" Fiona asked.

"Of course. It is the best way to get good at the sport," Miss Charlotte replied.

"Is that so? Well, I happen to think that you have to be completely bonkers to talk to your football," Fred blurted out scornfully.

It seemed Miss Charlotte had the power to block out any attempts to mock her. She beamed a smile at Fred before announcing: "Today every one of you will get to know your football."

She opened a big bag and took out dozens of footballs.

"Enjoy!" she shouted with a happy voice.

This time our coach did not train with us. She sat herself down in a corner of the gym

and took a book out of her pocket. When I happened to get close to her, I heard her pronounce these strange words: "Ah, how the snow has snowed! My window is a garden..."

That did not make any sense. But Billy, who happened to walk next to me, explained that Miss Charlotte was reciting a poem. By the Canadian poet Émile Nelligan. Billy Bungalow is a such a boffin! And Miss Charlotte is anything but boring!

Chapter 5

The Famous Professor Martinonini

An hour later, most children had given their ball a name. Martin and Eric played with theirs as if they were hacky sacks. Others were playing keepie-uppie using their chests, heads and backsides. Lying on their backs and chattering away, Fiona and her friends passed a ball to each other with their feet. And Laurence, who goes to circus lessons, was juggling three balls at the same time.

The funniest of all were the conversations.

"Kick Bilbo my way!"

"Catch King Kong for me, will you?"

"Let me bring Phoebe back to you."

"Have you seen Wilfred?"

The atmosphere was hilarious. And the weirdest thing of all was that Potato – that is what I called my ball – seemed more and more familiar. I almost found it normal to talk to it.

We were really having a *ball* when a hysterical scream rang out through the gym. It sounded like the scream of someone falling from the hundred-and-ninety-second floor of a skyscraper.

It was PP. Accompanied by Fred. The traitor! He had gone to look for our headmistress so she could see the rather unconventional training methods of Miss Charlotte for herself.

"Are you all hopping mad or what? Stop this circus right now!" the headmistress roared.

All the children who were present at the training session stopped in their tracks. The headmistress looked around the gym and her eye caught Miss Charlotte sitting in the back with her nose stuck in a poetry book.

"You! You are an impostor... I mean, an impostress... Erm, anyway, you are not a real coach. Or I am the tooth fairy!"

We all felt anxious. She was about to sack Miss Charlotte!

But Laurence saved the day with an improvised speech in defence of Miss Charlotte.

"My dear headmistress," he started, sounding super-serious and ever so polite. "You may be a little worried because we are speaking to our footballs. But it's nothing to worry about! Miss Charlotte's training methods are very, very, very... modern! They have recently been developed by the famous Professor Martinonini from the University of..."

He hesitated. But PP was so astonished that she did not notice.

"...the university of Rome, in Italy," Laurence continued. "The idea is to develop an... intimate relationship with your ball. To perform better. In order to... win!"

For a second, PP hesitated. Fortunately, Laurence had been clever enough to use two key words: perform and win. In the end, PP muttered some excuses, wished us good luck in our training session and vanished.

Fred was furious.

"You got your way this time, but PP will be back. And next time she will want to see a training schedule."

"A training schedule? That's too bad, because we don't have one..." Miss Charlotte admitted, turning towards me.

My mates noticed that Miss Charlotte was looking at me. All eyes were on me. Did they really think I of all people had a solution?

Suddenly I had a revelation. What we needed was a strategy. Like in a game of chess. And strategy is my forte. I don't know how Miss Charlotte had figured that one out, but never mind.

"Billy and me, we will take care of the training schedule," I announced, wondering if it was really me who had spoken.

Someone laughed out loud.

"Jeremy Catastrophe, the expert in strategy!" Fred Ferocio said in a mocking voice.

Normally I would have felt really hurt by this insult. But this time I followed Miss Charlotte's example. I built an invisible wall between Fred and myself. And to my great relief, his taunts did not hurt me any more.

Chapter 6

Pass Tadpole to Mexico

"You must be out of your mind," Billy complained all the way to my house.

I did not let that discourage me.

"You, Billy, are going to write a fake training schedule. Something like Reginald Robust's, with tons of exhausting exercises. Got it?"

"Sure, but what about you?"

"I will come up with a plan that will work for a team of rubbish footballers like you and me. A stra-te-gic plan!"

It was a cool idea, but after an hour of racking my brains I still had not come up with a brilliant strategy. I could just picture Fred Ferocio's laugh as he shouted: "Jeremy Catastrophe! What about your strategy? Jeremy Catastrophe! Have you ever seen anything so stupid?"

I also had to think about my dad. If I do not find a way of improving my game before the last match of the season, he will humiliate me in front of a huge crowd. I know he will, because I know what he is like. It would not be the first time either.

At matches my dad always gets really worked up. I am not sure he is even aware of it. He will start shouting: "Get a move on, Jeremy! Don't

just stand there daydreaming! Make a bit of an effort, for crying out loud!"

After a while, it gets worse. He begins to holler: "No! Not like that! That was rubbish!"

My dad's words always stick in my head for a long time afterwards. Especially that one word: rubbish, rubbish, rubbish, rubbish…

I was beginning to have that feeling in the pit of my stomach I get when I am scared or worried. But then I thought of Miss Charlotte. I was wondering what she would come up with. I imagined her beaming smile and pictured her jumping up and down on the pitch with excitement and talking to Anatole. I remembered us talking to our King Kongs and Kiwis in the gym. And then, at last, I had an idea.

I talked it through with Billy. He burst out laughing. But then, immediately afterwards, he congratulated me.

"You're a real genius, Jeremy."

The next day I presented my plan to my teammates when we were all assembled on the pitch.

"Our objective is simple. We have to destabilize the opponent, distract them, make them lose concentration… and make them forget we want to score goals."

They all looked at me like I had lost my mind. Except Miss Charlotte. Her eyes, which are as blue as the sky, gave me courage.

"Those who can will entertain the other team. When we were getting to know our footballs, Eric and Martin, for example, kept on doing tricks as if they were playing with hacky sacks."

I gave some more examples. I had seen Fiona balance a ball on her head. When Miss Barbie is not too busy swooning in front of Fred, she takes dance lessons. And I had been amazed at the juggling prowess of Laurence and his Tadpole. That's what he calls his football!

"So you want us to do some circus number, is that correct?" Fred grumbled.

I reassured him: "You, Fred, will be playing football. Don't you worry about that! Everyone knows you are the best. We could not do it without you. The aim of my strategy is to help you score more goals."

Fred opened his eyes wide and his jaw dropped, so that he looked like a guppy at feeding time.

"But around you, it will be like a circus, with people dancing and acting. From now on, we will call ourselves using the names of our footballs. And we will speak in code."

There was one more element we needed for it to work. Thinking about the last lesson we had had that day – geography – I explained:

"Let's say that our goal is… the Arctic, right here, at this end of the field. And our opponent's goal is the Antarctic, in the south, at the other end. In between the two, there are the Americas. Over here we have North America, which is closer to the Arctic. So our half of the field is North America. The other half is South America. All we need to do is learn some of the names of the countries and remember where they are on the map. So when Fiona shouts 'Pass Tadpole

to Mexico', *we* will know where to shoot the ball. But the other team will be totally confused!"

All the players applauded when they heard my plan. All the players except Fred, obviously.

"Woah! Wait a minute!" our star player said.

I immediately felt that something was wrong.

"Can Mr Jeremy the so-called expert in strategy perhaps explain the method he is going to use to select which players will play in the match?"

It was as if Fred had just poured icy water over us. In my head it went: rubbish, rubbish – you are rubbish, Jeremy. I had completely forgotten that for a normal game of football you need eleven players. Not one more.

Ever since Miss Charlotte had started coaching us, the number of players had almost tripled. She had accepted Billy, Nadia, Fiona, Eric, Monica and lots of other children on the team. Some played very well. Others less so.

Thanks to Miss Charlotte, all the players had a good time and everyone felt like they were part of the team. But on the day of the match, only eleven of us could play. There was nothing we could do about that. Those are the rules.

We turned to our coach. It was up to her to come up with a solution. And to be honest, I didn't see how it could be solved!

Miss Charlotte did not say a word. And yet she did not seem to be at all disheartened.

"So, Miss Celery Stick, what are we going to do?" said Fred, challenging Miss Charlotte. "Do we dress up the players we don't need as ghosts? Do we cover them in invisible paint?"

Miss Charlotte burst out laughing. As if Fred had told her the best joke in the world.

"No, no… Let's see. It's very simple. There is a great solution."

We were all hanging on her lips. What would she come up with this time? Miss Charlotte was waiting for us to guess the answer. But no one had one.

"The day of the match we will organize a draw to select the players. A bit like bingo or the lottery!" she declared, raising her shoulders and putting her hands up, as if to say: we could have thought about that earlier.

Chapter 7

A Bit of Spling, Please

A draw! We were shocked.

"I have a better idea," Fred announced. "We pick the best eleven players... and sack the coach!"

All eyes were on Miss Charlotte again. She was neither angry nor insulted. She continued stroking Anatole and calmly looked at us.

"So, what's it going to be?" Fred asked. "Shall we select a proper winning team or get trounced?"

"That depends on what we want the most," Priti said. "Do we want to win the match or do we want everyone to get a chance?"

We all started to speak at the same time. Opinions were divided. Eric pointed out that the idea of a match really is to win.

"If not, it would be no different from a training session," he blurted out.

Most of the players seemed to agree. Fred saw his chance to have a vote. Miss Charlotte still was not saying anything.

In front of me, Billy was nervously chewing on a toffee. I had noticed he had been eating a lot less of them lately. I also knew he had been going for runs in the morning since he joined the team.

Billy did everything he could to improve his game. He dreamt of being given the chance to play. The same was true for Nadia, whom we all called the flea because she was the smallest pupil of the class. Thanks to Miss Charlotte, Nadia had discovered she had a real talent for football.

"Why don't you say something," I asked our coach.

She gave a start. It was as if she had been somewhere far away. She looked at us with her sky-blue eyes. Then she began to talk.

"Anatole and I have won lots of trophies," she began. "Is that not true, Anatole? But one day, something happened… And we understood. That is all."

"What happened?" Laurence wanted to know.

"And what was it that you understood?" Fiona added.

"We understood that the most important thing is to have *spling*," Miss Charlotte explained, ignoring Laurence's question.

A number of pupils shouted in chorus.

"To have *what*?"

Miss Charlotte giggled.

"*Spling* is... enjoyment. The pleasure of playing. A passion for football. The joy of giving it your all. And not just so you can win. The goal is to play well."

There was something exciting and at the same time comforting in the words of our coach. We were spellbound.

"For me and for Anatole," Miss Charlotte continued, "the best team is not the one which scores the most goals. It is the team that has the most passion, the most enthusiasm, the most positive energy."

"Sure, sure. Enough of speeches now," Fred interrupted. "It is time to vote."

We held a secret vote so that no one would be embarrassed, and we all wrote down what we wanted on a little bit of paper. Then Priti and Monica counted the votes.

Each of us was wondering how the other had voted. Shortly afterwards, Monica stepped forwards to read out the result.

"Three... against twenty-three," she announced.

We were all eager to get more details. Three for what?

"Three in favour of Fred's idea and twenty-three in favour of Miss Charlotte's," Monica explained.

I felt as if I were sprouting wings. I was so happy. Until Fred uttered two shocking short sentences.

"That's it: I quit. I am no longer part of this team," he declared as he stormed off.

Chapter 8

The Answer Is in the Sky

We were shattered.

"What a disaster!" Mélodie groaned.

"Now we really are in a massive pickle," Martin concluded. "They're going to destroy us."

"The best thing to do is to cancel the match. After all, what do we care if their school will be named after Tony Brilliant?" Fiona said.

Her proposal made sense. The more you thought about it, the more it looked like the obvious thing to do. As far as we were concerned...

"Cancel the match?! Never!" Miss Charlotte suddenly shouted. "Why? It will be absolutely… fabulous!"

The worst thing was that she actually believed it too. Her face lit up, and she looked pleased as Punch.

"How? Don't you understand?" Martin let out, impatient. "It's Fred who scores nearly all our goals. So tell us, how will we cope without him?"

Miss Charlotte was no longer listening. She was looking at the sky, where a flight of birds was passing over.

"Canada geese," Billy whispered in my ear.

Then our coach finally remembered we were still waiting for a response. But instead of reassuring us, she simply said: "The answer is in the sky."

And whoosh! Off she went.

Chapter 9

Grasshopper Juice for All

The next day we all felt depressed when we came to the training. Fiona had news about Fred. Disastrous news! The traitor was going to play for our rivals! His mother lives in Black Duck Brook and his father in Blueberry Bay, so he can play for whichever team he wants – he is perfectly entitled to do so.

We were done for. In a pickle. Up the creek. Our opponents were going to make mincemeat of us.

"What you need is a little pick-me-up," Miss Charlotte decided when she saw us walk onto the field.

She opened her bag and took out a couple of flasks.

"Smalalamiam for everyone!"

We all queued up, like they do in Asterix when the druid Getafix dishes out his magic potion. While we were waiting our turn, we were all trying to guess what Miss Charlotte put in her drink. No one had dared to ask. We all guessed it was a secret. Laurence, who likes to come out with silly comments, suggested it was probably a mixture of fruit juice and… wee!

We all had our ration. It had a strange and at the same time wonderful taste. We all agreed that smalalamiam was delicious.

"And? Have you found the answer in the sky?" Miss Charlotte asked finally.

Billy put his hand up, as if he were in class.

"To win, we must do like the geese," he answered, sounding very sure of himself.

No one understood what he was going on about, so he explained.

"Geese manage to fly fast and for a long time because they take turns. They form a big V so they can cope with headwinds. The birds up front have to work the hardest, but as soon as they get too tired, they are replaced by others who are less tired."

"OK… but what does *that* have to do with football?" Miranda wanted to know.

"What has it got to do with football?" Miss Charlotte cried out enthusiastically. "Helping each other, of course! If the geese were to fly by themselves, they would not get anywhere. They only succeed because they stick together."

It was genius. I was proud of our coach.

"Miss Charlotte is right," I added. "None of us could replace Fred individually. But if we stick together, we might have a chance. We have to change positions all the time and pass the ball around a lot. We must all do the best we can."

We decided to give it a try. There and then, in spite of the fact that it began to drizzle. At the start, we all ran with the ball as far as we could without passing it to anyone. That was how we had always done it. But then, little by little, our way of playing changed. When Monica passed me the ball, I ran as quick as a flash with ball. And then I passed it to Eric, who passed it to Fiona, who passed it to Laurence and… we scored! A real team effort!

From that day on, all the players were making huge progress. Was it because of the smalalamiam that Miss Charlotte gave us before each training session? Was it her geese-based strategy? Or our distraction techniques?

We continued to have fun and kept guessing what Miss Charlotte put in her magic drink. No yak milk, that was for sure! From time to time, Fiona told us about Fred and his team. We all understood that love was in the air for Fred and Fiona.

The early signs indicated that Fred was not all that happy playing for our rivals. Fiona told us that the coach, Reginald Robust, never stopped shouting. He was never pleased and never encouraging.

With us, it was the opposite. With Miss Charlotte we never felt like we were rubbish or useless. Except the day when Martin called Eric a numpty...

Martin was just winding Eric up in order to make it easier to take the ball off him. But Eric responded by calling Martin an idiot. And they got into a fight. Business as usual.

Except that when Miss Charlotte saw this, it was as if she had frozen solid or as if someone had taken the batteries out of her. She stood there without moving a muscle. Like a statue. We got so scared that Laurence separated the two fighting boys.

Miss Charlotte returned to normal – almost, because it was as if something had died inside her. She made a few steps and then announced that the training session was over, even though we had only just started!

Before she left, she told Eric: "Next time, do not waste your anger. Turn it into something positive."

Eric did not understand. Once again, Billy had to explain: "Next time, instead of hitting Martin on the head, hit the ball into the back of the net."

The next day, Miss Charlotte was her old self again. As for us, we knew that fights were out of the question. In Miss Charlotte's rule book, harmony was more important than the number of players.

A week later there was another moment of drama. An even worse one. We had split the team in two and were playing against each other. Billy and I were on the bench and looked on. We were far from disappointed, though, because it was a fantastic match.

As Nadia was running across the field, someone shouted: "King Kong to Quebec."

Pierre got the ball and wanted to pass it to Laurence. Eric tried to intercept the ball, but Laurence started doing keepie-uppies. It was quite a sight! He was so good that we all forgot about the match and applauded him.

That is when the storm broke out. Not in the sky, but on the football pitch.

It happened when PP arrived.

Chapter 10

Miss Charlotte's Secret

The anger of our headmistress was like a hurricane. She went straight for Miss Charlotte.

"You gnarled old turnip! You numbskull! You big old twit!" she roared at the top of her voice as she stormed towards our football coach.

Miss Charlotte was waiting for her. She did not seem in the least intimidated. She rather looked as if she felt sorry for PP.

Our headmistress was only a few centimetres away from Miss Charlotte's face and still hurling abuse at her. At that point our coach did something that surprised us all. Again!

"Poor old thing!" Miss Charlotte exclaimed, looking at Paulette Pesky.

Our coach looked very intently at our headmistress, and there was something in her eyes that spoke of... tenderness. Yes, I think that is the word I am looking for.

PP's anger subsided. Our headmistress just seemed sad. And lost.

Miss Charlotte opened her arms wide.

And then, believe or not, PP threw herself into Miss Charlotte's arms. Not to hit her or to hurt her. But to be comforted!

Our headmistress was sobbing like a child.

"Boohoo! Sniff sniff. Boohoohoo. Sniff sniff. Boohoo!"

Miss Charlotte led PP to some bushes at the far end of the pitch. We appointed Fiona as our spy to see what was going on. When she came back after a while, she told us everything. What a story! Grown-ups can be pretty messed up sometimes!

Paulette Pesky confessed to Miss Charlotte that she wanted to win at all cost. She was

not that bothered about the school being renamed after Tony Brilliant. What she really wanted above everything else was to beat her sister.

Yvette and Paulette are twins. No one knows who was born first. Yvette swears it was her, while Paulette says the opposite is true. Ever since they were born, each one of them has always wanted to be the first, the most beautiful, the best.

Our coach listened to our headmistress for a long time. When PP seemed to feel a little better, Miss Charlotte gave her a secret tip. A tip that completely transformed Paulette Pesky.

"You don't need to compete with your sister," Miss Charlotte explained to her. "You don't have to be the best. You are unique. That is enough."

At first PP stared at Miss Charlotte as if her face were green and she had antennae coming out of her head. Then, little by little, a shy smile began to spread across her face until in the end it turned into a huge grin. She looked at Miss Charlotte as if she had just achieved the impossible.

As Fiona was telling all that, I heard a noise behind us. It was Fred. The Blueberry Bay traitor had become a spy as well!

I watched him sneak off quietly. No one else had seen him.

I wondered if Fred had heard Miss Charlotte's secret tip. And what he might think of it.

Chapter 11

An Almighty Big Kick!

The morning of the big match I was so nervous that when I finished breakfast I put the milk in the cupboard and the cereal in the fridge. I was about to leave when my dad told me: "Good luck, my son. Have a great match…"

I was really hoping he would leave it at that. That there would be no threats and pressure this time. But no! He added: "Try not to embarrass me! If you do…"

He paused and thought for a bit before continuing: "If you do, I will take it upon myself to train you during the holidays. And

believe me, you *will* learn to score goals or my
name is not Roger!"

I felt crushed by my dad's threat. I would never
survive a summer like that. Then I realized that
I might not even be playing that day. Little did
my dad know. Maybe I would be lucky and not
get selected…

When I arrived on the pitch, Laurence cried
out: "Everyone is here. We can start the draw."

Miss Charlotte plunged her hand into a bag
that contained little cards with our names on.

Poor Billy! He didn't make the draw. I on the
other hand did.

I felt a little discouraged because my dad
would be there. If it weren't for him, I would
probably have been delighted to play.

Even before the start of the match, the difference
between the two teams was obvious. While we
were gorging ourselves on smalalamiam – no one
had discovered the secret ingredients yet! – the
members of the other team were pulling faces
as they swallowed their yak milk. Then, to help
us relax, Miss Charlotte gave us a riddle.

"What is invisible and smells of bananas?"

While we were laughing at the solution (a monkey's fart!), the other team was exhausting itself by running around the pitch. And while Miss Charlotte showed us how to give massages and repeated how important it was to play well and have a good time, Reginald Robust yelled at his team: "You are here to win! Get it into your thick skulls!"

His voice was threatening and his stare terrifying. Standing next to him, Yvette Pesky was not much more encouraging. I would rather spend a whole day tidying my bedroom than be on their team.

At last the match began. Our opponents were on great form. They kicked the ball as if their lives depended on it. However hard Pierre, our goalie, ran to and fro and jumped up and down to make saves, the other team quickly scored three goals.

Suddenly someone shouted: "Phoebe to Florida!"

And then: "King Kong to Quebec!"

Something magical happened. We felt like one. And this boosted our energy.

We made more and more passes until Fiona got the ball. The crowd was impressed when she did a pirouette, balancing the ball on her head. Many parents were wondering what that was about, but they were captivated nevertheless.

Meanwhile, what do you think Miss Charlotte was doing? She was knitting! Yes, knitting! She was knitting like mad, making a scarf that was already so long it should be in the

Guinness World Records. The further the match progressed, the faster her knitting needles were clicking. It was a quite a spectacle. At one point, I saw Fred looking her way. He was dumbstruck, but I could almost have sworn he smiled.

The other team appeared to be more and more discombobulated. While Laurence was showing off his acrobatic tricks, they were so distracted that we were able to score our first goal. And, not long after that, our second one.

The team from Blueberry Bay were up four goals to two when the ball grazed my head.

"Wake up Jeremy! You're not in bed!" my dad shouted, loud enough for everyone to hear.

I was upset and angry. I looked for my dad in the crowd. My eyes met those of Miss Charlotte. Next to her I recognized PP. She was completely transformed and smiled like never before. I also spotted Marie, my dearest cousin and friend. That comforted me.

Then someone shouted: "Potato to Ontario!"

And Eric passed to me. The ball had almost reached me when I heard: "Get a move on, Jeremy!"

My dad again.

Smoke was starting to come out of my ears when I remembered Miss Charlotte's advice: turn your anger into something positive.

I took a step back and then booted the ball with all my strength. It was an almighty kick!

The crowd cheered like mad. I had just scored a goal! For the first time in my life!

After that, it all went very fast. Fiona had just intercepted the ball when a player of the other team, a huge gorilla of a guy, tackled her. Fiona fell hard and could not get up.

Play was stopped. Fiona was hurt. She had sprained her ankle. The poor thing was unable to walk. So we had to find a sub.

The worst thing was that the referee didn't say anything. And instead of telling his gorilla off, Reginald Robust patted him on the back. I know, because I saw it with my own eyes. I also saw Fred protest to his coach, making wild gestures.

Our team gathered round Miss Charlotte and her leather bag, which contained the little slips of papers with our names on. A storm was brewing. We were very angry with the player who had tackled Fiona, and also with the referee, who had not done anything.

Miss Charlotte was about to dip her hand into the bag when someone shouted: "No! Wait!"

It was Fred. He wanted to rejoin our team. He'd had enough of Reginald Robust and the gorilla who had hurt his sweetheart.

Laurence wrote Fred's name on a bit of paper. There was a lot of tension. We all really wanted to crush our rivals. Everyone wanted Fred to be selected. Everyone except, maybe, Billy. He was still hoping he might at last have a chance to play.

Miss Charlotte plunged her hand in the bag and took out a little slip of paper. She unfolded it and read: "Fred Ferocio!"

For a short while I thought she had done it on purpose, that it was no coincidence she had picked Fred. But I did not have much time to think it over, because Fred roared: "We're going to thrash them!"

Chapter 12

Goals and Kisses

No one moved. Something in Fred's tone had struck us. Miss Charlotte did not say a word, but we could all see what she was thinking. The expression on her face told us that all those weeks of training, all those litres of smalalamiam should not have led to this.

Not far from us, Fiona was sitting on a bench, with her leg up and a bag of ice on her ankle. Fred looked at her for a moment before speaking to Miss Charlotte.

"Do you have a better suggestion?" he asked, almost sounding polite.

"The best revenge would be for you all to have a really, really good time!" Miss Charlotte replied.

Her words struck a chord in my heart.

"She's right. Instead of behaving ourselves like them, we should show them how you can have fun on the pitch."

"And, Fred? What do you think?" Fiona asked, smiling warmly and her eyes shining.

"Well... OK then!" said Fred. "We'll show them that as well as being good players we can also have fun."

Miss Charlotte was right. It turned into a fabulous match. Monica sang bits from her favourite song as she was dribbling the ball with her feet. Nicholas surprised everyone by doing two backflips, while Theo made a spectacular jump. Fred made a couple of surging runs across the pitch, beating all his opponents. And the players from Black Duck Brook kept on shouting out their secret codes as they were passing the ball around.

We had a whale of a time. We laughed and jumped and shouted. And Fred scored a goal too. But most of all, we had a really, really good time. The other team seemed more and more demoralized. As if our joy depressed them. Maybe they realized they did not understand the true beauty of the game.

The scores were tied now. All we needed was for Fred to hit the back of the net and we would win the match.

"Go, Fred, go!" Fiona encouraged him from the stands.

Fred turned around to look at his sweetheart. As he was looking over, his eyes caught sight of Billy. Then Fred dashed towards the ball… and let himself fall flat on his face.

Play was stopped again. No one understood what had just happened.

Fred got up. He did not even pretend to limp. He walked straight up to Billy.

"Here you are! It's your turn now," he said, taking off his shirt to give it to Billy.

It was clear what was going on. Fred was not hurt at all. He just wanted to give Billy a chance!

Billy Bungalow could not believe what was happening to him.

"Go on! Get a move on, before I change my mind," Fred mumbled, pushing Billy towards the pitch.

Our rivals perked up when they found out that Fred had been replaced. They came awfully close to scoring the winning goal. Pierre was only just able to stop the ball.

Then a voice rang out from the stands. A voice we had not heard before.

"Go on, Billy! You can do it!" shouted Miss Charlotte with unshakable confidence.

Three minutes later Billy sent the ball into the back of the net.

We had won! The crowd went mad and Billy was on cloud nine. I have never seen anyone so happy in my whole life. While we were jumping up and down like monkeys to express our joy, Fred walked over to Fiona. And when he got there, he kissed her on the cheek, in front of everyone!

Epilogue

Our headmistress congratulated us very warmly. She invited us to choose a new name for the school. No one was bothered about naming it after Tony Brilliant. Laurence had a better idea: "The Smalalamiam Academy!" he suggested.

Fiona used this moment to get Miss Charlotte to reveal the secret of her smalalamiam. We had worked out that it contained peach juice, honey, crushed hazelnuts and caramel, but there was at least one ingredient missing, which would explain why it was so effective.

"You still haven't figured it out?" Miss Charlotte said, astonished. "The secret ingredient is *spling*!"

My dad came over to congratulate me. He gave me a pat on the back, saying: "I knew I would make a good striker out of you!"

I looked at my dad. He was proud of me. Not because I had given it my all, but because I had scored a goal.

It all became clear to me. I plucked up my courage and told my dad: "I will never be a great striker, Dad. I enjoy playing, that's all. But I am brilliant at strategy. Next year I will be the assistant coach."

My dad did not reply. I think he was too surprised at seeing me so full of determination.

Marie was waiting for me in the stands. Alone. In her hand she was holding a pebble.

"I would like you to meet Gertrude," she said, sounding emotional.

My cousin Marie explained that Gertrude was more than just a little stone. Miss Charlotte had told it her deepest secrets. Marie had been looking after it for quite a while now. So *that* was the precious object she had spoken about before in such a mysterious tone.

"Miss Charlotte was keen to see it again," Marie continued. "But then she decided you should have it for a while. She told me to hand it over to you…"

It took a while before it sank in.

"You mean to say that she's gone?"

Marie nodded.

I felt abandoned and lost. All of a sudden I discovered just how much our football coach had come to mean to me.

Marie understood what I was going through. She opened my hand and put Gertrude in it. I immediately felt there was something of Miss Charlotte in that pebble.

I talk to Gertrude a lot. Especially when my dad is putting pressure on me. Gertrude

reminds me of what Miss Charlotte used to say. And it reminds me that I don't need to be the best. I am unique. And that is enough.

Miss Charlotte is right. I know it.

Like I know that one day, very soon perhaps, she will reappear in my life.

IF YOU LIKED THIS STORY, WHY DON'T YOU TRY ANOTHER OF MISS CHARLOTTE'S ADVENTURES?

"She's bonkers!"

Miss Charlotte, the new teacher, is not like the others: she wears a large hat and a crumpled dress that make her look like a scarecrow, and she talks to a rock. The children think she is crazy at first, but soon realize she makes school more fun, getting them to measure the room with cooked spaghetti in maths class, telling fascinating stories about a gorilla and even taking the pupils on at football.

The first book in Dominique Demers's popular series, *The New Teacher* - brilliantly illustrated by Tony Ross - is an entertaining, imaginative and inspiring book that will make you wish you had a teacher just like Miss Charlotte.

"That beanpole of a woman!"

When the mysterious and eccentric Miss Charlotte arrives in the village of Saint-Anatole to take over the tiny library, the locals are surprised to find out that she does things differently. Wearing a long blue dress and a giant hat, she takes her books out for a walk in a wheelbarrow and shows the children that reading can be fun and useful. Sometimes she is so caught up in the magic of the stories she shares with her audience that she forgets all sense of reality - so much so that one day she loses consciousness and the children must find a way to bring her back.

The second in Dominique Demers's popular series, *The Mysterious Librarian*, brilliantly illustrated by Tony Ross, is a wonderful story about the magical and inspiring power of books.